Monster Boy and the Halloween Parade

BY CARL EMERSON
ILLUSTRATED BY LON LEVIN

visit us at www.abdopublishing.com

Published by Magic Wagon, a division of the ABDO Group, 8000 West 78th Street, Edina, Minnesota 55439.
Copyright © 2011 by Abdo Consulting Group, Inc. International copyrights reserved in all countries. All rights reserved. No part of this book may be reproduced in any form without written permission from the publisher.

Looking Glass Library™ is a trademark and logo of Magic Wagon.

Printed in the United States of America, North Mankato, Minnesota.
052010
092010

Text by Carl Emerson
Illustrations by Lon Levin
Edited by Nadia Higgins
Interior layout and design by Emily Love
Cover design by Emily Love

Library of Congress Cataloging-in-Publication Data
Emerson, Carl.
  Monster Boy and the Halloween parade / by Carl Emerson ; illustrated by Lon Levin.
    p. cm. — (Monster Boy)
  ISBN 978-1-60270-777-1
  [1. Monsters—Fiction. 2. Halloween—Fiction. 3. Costume—Fiction.] I. Levin, Lon, ill. II. Title.
  PZ7.E582Mnt 2010
  [E]—dc22
                        2010007078

It was a math quiz day. Miss Taken was making sure that her students were keeping their eyes on their own papers.

Marty Onster felt a ball of paper bounce off his head just as Miss Taken passed his desk.

"Hey, Monster Boy!" Bart Ully whispered. "What did you get for number three?"

Marty refused to turn and look at Bart. He did not want to help Bart cheat, and he did not like being called Monster Boy.

"OK, children," Miss Taken said at last. "Time to put down your pencils and pass your papers forward."

Bart threw his pencil down. "Five blanks!
I'll get you for this, Onster!"

Meanwhile, Miss Taken was trying to get everyone's attention.

"I have an exciting announcement!" she called out. "You may wear your costumes to school tomorrow for Halloween. And we will have a parade through the hallways at recess time."

All the kids cheered, except for Bart. He just smirked like he had some big, evil secret.

That night, Marty worked hard to finish his costume.

"Marty!" his mother called. "I have your costume ready! I bought some fang extenders, extra slobber, and oozy, schmoozy slime!"

But Marty already had his costume figured out. Sally Weet, his best friend, was going to be Power Girl. And he was going to be Mega Boy.

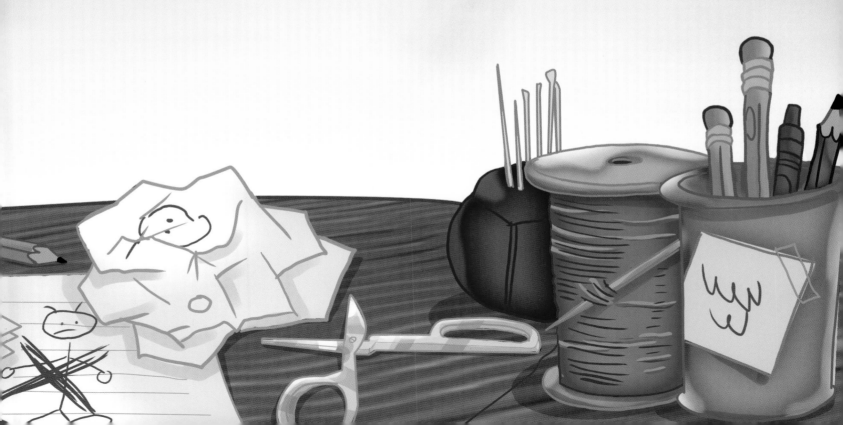

"Mega Boy is the most awesome, most amazing boy in the whole world!" Marty said.

"But Marty, he's not a monster," said Marty's dad. "He's not even a little bit scary, and he has never eaten a child."

Marty groaned. His parents always wanted him to be more monster-y.

The next morning, Marty carefully stuffed his Mega Boy costume into his backpack. Then, he dressed up as a monster, just like his parents wanted.

"Oh no! What are you wearing?" Sally asked when she saw Marty at school.

"Don't worry, Sally," Marty said. Then he darted into the bathroom and came out dressed as his favorite superhero.

"Awesome!" shouted Sally.

As class was starting, Bart walked in dressed as . . . Bart. He bumped into Marty's desk on purpose on his way to his seat. "Nice costume," Bart sneered. "I stopped liking Mega Boy when I was, like, four."

Marty felt his skin warming up. Little hairs popped up on the back of his neck. He took a deep breath. If he got too mad, he'd turn into a real monster. That was the *last* thing he wanted today.

"At least we're wearing costumes," Sally said to Bart.

"Just wait until the parade," Bart shot back. "Then you'll see my real costume!"

When it was time for the parade, Bart asked for a hall pass and went to the bathroom to change.

Bart came back in twirling around
and waving his arms.

"Ha-ha!" he shouted. "Look at me! I'm Onster, the Monster Boy! I drool like a baby. Want to pet my fur? Oh no, watch out! You don't want to get fleas!"

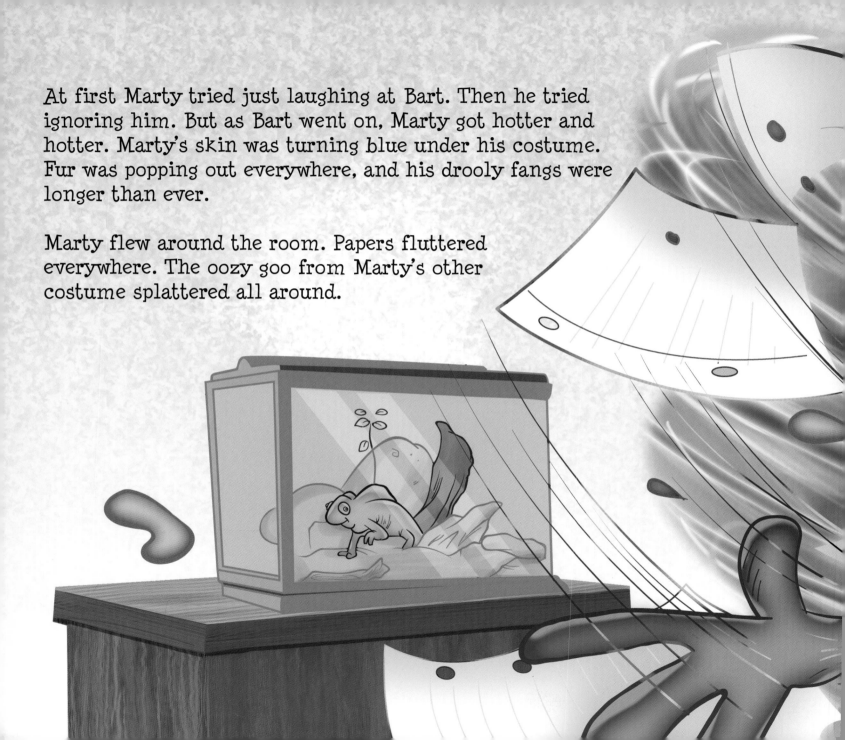

At first Marty tried just laughing at Bart. Then he tried ignoring him. But as Bart went on, Marty got hotter and hotter. Marty's skin was turning blue under his costume. Fur was popping out everywhere, and his drooly fangs were longer than ever.

Marty flew around the room. Papers fluttered everywhere. The oozy goo from Marty's other costume splattered all around.

When it was over, Marty sat
panting in the corner.

"Bart Ully!" Miss Taken shouted.
"You clean up this mess at once!"

"But I—," Bart started to say. "It wasn't me."

"Nice try, Mr. Ully," Miss Taken said. "But I saw you with my own eyes."

Sally smiled at Marty. "It looks like Mega Boy did it again!"

Contain Your Inner Monster
Tips from Marty Onster

Superheroes don't worry about what other people think. Neither should you!

When someone makes you mad, you don't have to get all blue and hairy. Take a deep breath, and maybe you won't turn into a monster.

Focus on your friends. Remember that true friends will stand by you even when you behave like a monster.